SHERLOCK CHICK AND THE GIANT EGG MYSTERY

by Robert Quackenbush

PARENTS MAGAZINE PRESS · NEW YORK

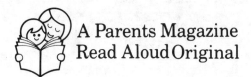

A Parents Magazine
Read Aloud Original

Library of Congress Cataloging-in-Publication Data

Quackenbush, Robert M.
  Sherlock Chick and the giant egg mystery/by Robert Quackenbush.
    p.   cm.

  Summary: Sherlock Chick tries to solve the mystery of the
giant egg that arrives at the farm.
  ISBN 0–8193–1178–2
  [1. Chickens—Fiction. 2. Eggs—Fiction. 3. Farm life—
Fiction. 4. Mystery and detective stories.]   I. Title.
PZ7.Q16Sjm   1989
[E]—dc19
                                                    88–4093
                                                       CIP
                                                        AC

ISBN 0–8193–1178–2

For Piet

Sherlock Chick,
the great detective,
was out walking one day
when he saw a big box.
"I wonder what this could be,"
he said.

Along came Sherlock Chick's
friends, Squeakins Mouse
and Charlie Chipmunk.
"What's in the box?"
they asked.

Just then, one side
of the box plopped open.
Out rolled a giant egg!

Sherlock Chick and his
friends were surprised.
"What kind of egg is that?"
asked Charlie Chipmunk.
"I don't know,"
said Sherlock Chick.
"I'll go get my mother.
She knows about eggs."
He ran to the chicken coop
to find Emma Hen.

"My goodness!" said Emma Hen.
"I've never seen such a big egg.
It needs warming so whatever
is inside can hatch.
A mother knows these things."
She climbed up on the
egg and sat down.

"This isn't going to work,"
said Emma Hen.
"The egg is much too big
for me to keep warm
all by myself."
"We'll help you!"
said Squeakins Mouse
and Charlie Chipmunk.
They climbed up on
the egg with her.

While the three of them
were busy on the egg,
Sherlock Chick went
to have another look
at the box.
He was hoping to
find some clues.
He wanted to solve the
mystery of the giant egg.

Sherlock Chick walked
around the box.
On the back he found a label.
Now he knew that the egg
was for Farmer Jones.
And he knew it came from
Aunt Matilda in Africa.

Further along, Sherlock Chick
saw four stamps.
One showed a lion.
One showed a gorilla.
One showed an elephant.
And one stamp was torn.
All that could be seen were
two feet and the letters "ich."
"Hmmm," said Sherlock Chick.
"I wonder what an *ich* is."

Sherlock Chick went back
to the others.
"I found out that the egg
came from Africa," he said.
"And there were stamps on
the box showing a lion,
a gorilla, and an elephant."
Squeakins, Charlie, and
Emma Hen gasped.
"What if there's a lion
inside the egg?" said Squeakins.
"Or a gorilla?" said Emma Hen.
"Or an elephant?" said Charlie.

"Lions! Gorillas! Elephants!"
shouted Emma Hen.
"Run for your lives!"
yelled Squeakins.
They all jumped off
the egg and ran.

"Come back!" said
Sherlock Chick.
"Lions, gorillas, and elephants
don't hatch from eggs.
Besides, I also saw a
stamp with an animal
called an ich."

"My boy!" said Emma Hen.
"Of course you are right
about the other animals.
But what in the world
is an ich?"
"It makes me feel like
scratching," said Squeakins.
"That's an itch,"
said Sherlock Chick.
"If we all keep warming
the egg, perhaps we will
find out what is inside."
This time, Sherlock
sat on the egg, too.

They sat on the egg
for a long time.
Then Emma Hen said,
"I feel something moving."
The others felt it, too.

The egg was cracking open.
The four sitters
jumped off at once.
And in the nick
of time, too!
The shell broke apart
and out came...

...A *giant* baby bird!

"My goodness!" said Emma Hen.

"What a big ich!"

Sherlock Chick studied the bird.

Then he remembered a picture

he had seen in one of his books.

"This bird is not an ich!"

he said.

"Then what is it?"

asked the others.

"This bird is a baby ostrich,"
said Sherlock Chick.
"Only the last three letters
of his name were on the stamp.
The rest of his name
was torn off."

"What a smart detective
you are!"
said Emma Hen.
"And won't Farmer Jones be
surprised when he sees
the baby ostrich,"
said Squeakins.
"No more than us,"
said Sherlock Chick.
"After all...

...we hatched him!"

About the Author

Robert Quackenbush was thinking about
how children are surprised and delighted
by presents—the unexpected box, the
mysterious contents—when he heard that
many farmers are looking for new things to
raise. "What might they grow?" wondered
Mr. Quackenbush. So Sherlock Chick
provided an answer.

Robert Quackenbush, an international
author and illustrator of over 150 books for
children, created the popular *Henry the
Duck* series for Parents. He has received
many honors for his work, including an
Edgar Allan Poe Special Award for best
children's mystery. In addition to creating
picture books, Mr. Quackenbush owns an
art gallery in New York City, where he
teaches writing and illustrating to children
and adults.

Sherlock Chick and the Giant Egg Mystery
is the third book in Mr. Quackenbush's
popular *Sherlock Chick* mystery series.